Magic Kitten

Starry Sticker and Activity Book

Material originally published as *Magic Kitten Activity Annual*, 2009. Copyright © Puffin Books, 2008, 2009. Based on the Magic Kitten series, copyright © Sue Bentley. Illustrations © Andrew Farley, Angela Swan, 2006, 2007, 2008, 2009. First printed in Great Britain in 2009 by Penguin Books Ltd. as *Magic Kitten Purrfect Fun Bumper Activity Book*. First published in the United States in 2013 by Grosset & Dunlap, a division of Penguin Young Readers Group, 345 Hudson Street, New York, New York 10014. GROSSET & DUNLAP is a trademark of Penguin Group (USA) Inc. Manufactured in China.

ISBN 978-0-448-46581-4

10 9 8 7 6 5 4 3 2 1

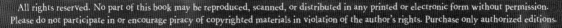

ALWAYS LEARNING

PEARSON

MISSING!

Flame

Have you seen this kitten?

Flame is a magic kitten of royal blood who is missing from his own world. His uncle Ebony wants to make sure Flame is found quickly. Flame may be hard to spot, since he often appears in a variety of fluffy kitten colors, but you can recognize him by his big emerald eyes and whiskers that crackle with magic!

He is believed to be looking for a young friend to take care of him.

Could it be you?

If you find this very special kitten, please let Ebony, ruler of the Lion Throne, know.

Who Is Flame?

Prince Flame, a young white lion, is heir to the Lion Throne,
but he is not yet strong enough to stand up to his evil uncle Ebony,
who has claimed the throne as his own.

With the help of his friend and adviser, an old gray lion named Cirrus, Flame is
hiding in the human world disguised as a kitten until he can challenge Ebony for
the throne. However, he doesn't risk staying in one place for too long, since his
uncle's spies are everywhere and are desperate to find him.

Flame magically appears in the lives of his new young friends, traveling from
family to family in various kitten guises. He puts his magic powers to good
use while living with his human companions, helping those who help him— but
as soon as he senses that his enemies are close, he must leave. Transformed back
into a majestic white lion, with Cirrus at his side, Flame returns to the Lion
Kingdom—until his next magical visit to our world . . .

My Purrfect Kitten

All kittens are adorable, but everyone has their purrsonal favorite.
Is yours a sweet silver tabby, a playful Persian, or a cute calico kitten?

This is my purrfect kitten:

Breed: . . . .

Male/female: . . . .

Coat color: . . . .

Short-haired/long-haired: . . . .

Eye color: . . . .

Personality: . . . .

. . . .

. . . .

. . . .

Draw your
purrfect
kitten here.

My kitten would be called: . . . .

Its favorite place to sleep would be: . . . .

. . . .

Its favorite toys would be: . . . .

. . . .

These are the games we would play together: . . . .

. . . .

. . . .

Flame and Friends

Color these pictures of Flame helping Lisa do the dishes, going for a ride with Zoe, and riding on a boat with Kim.

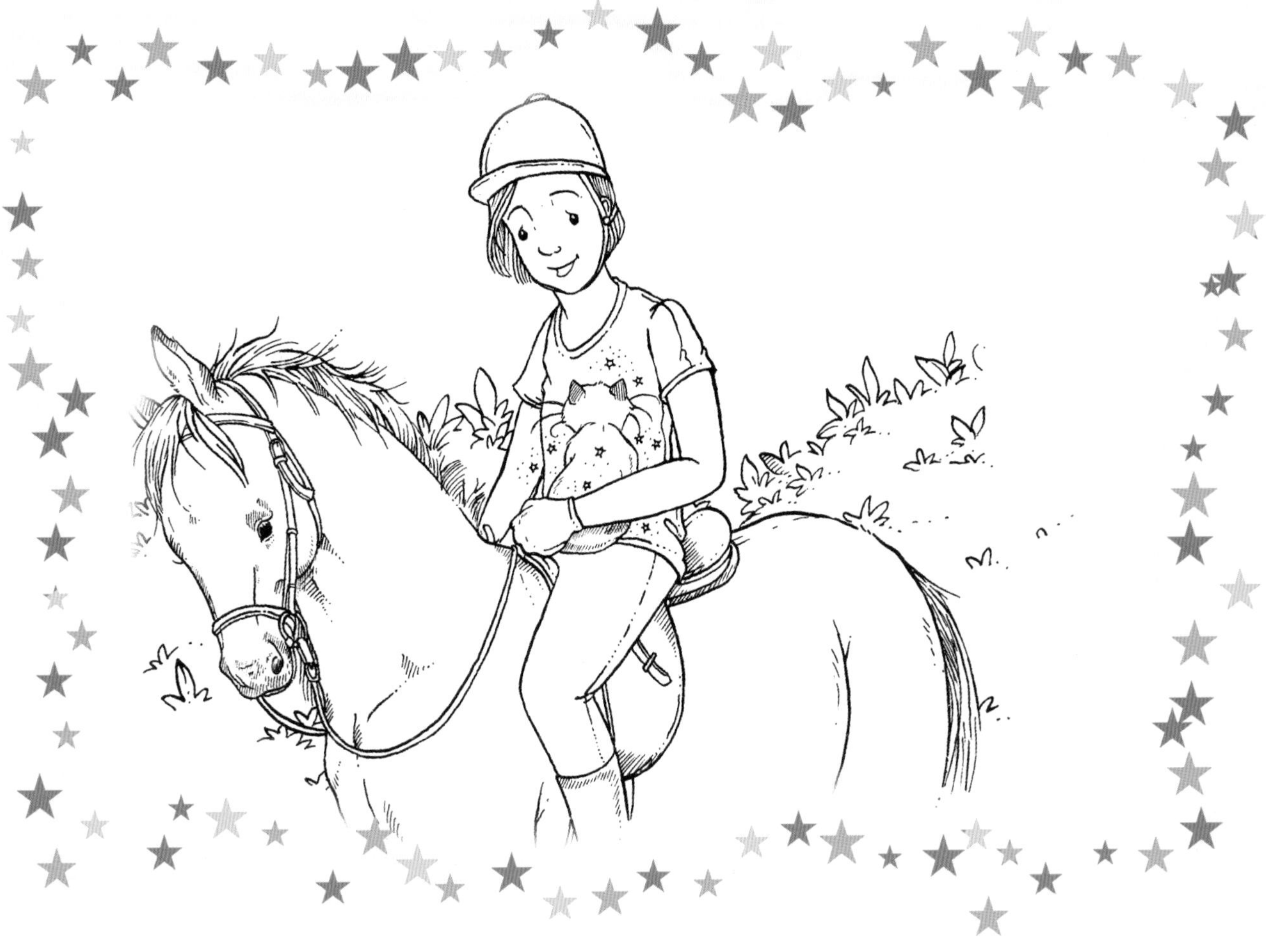

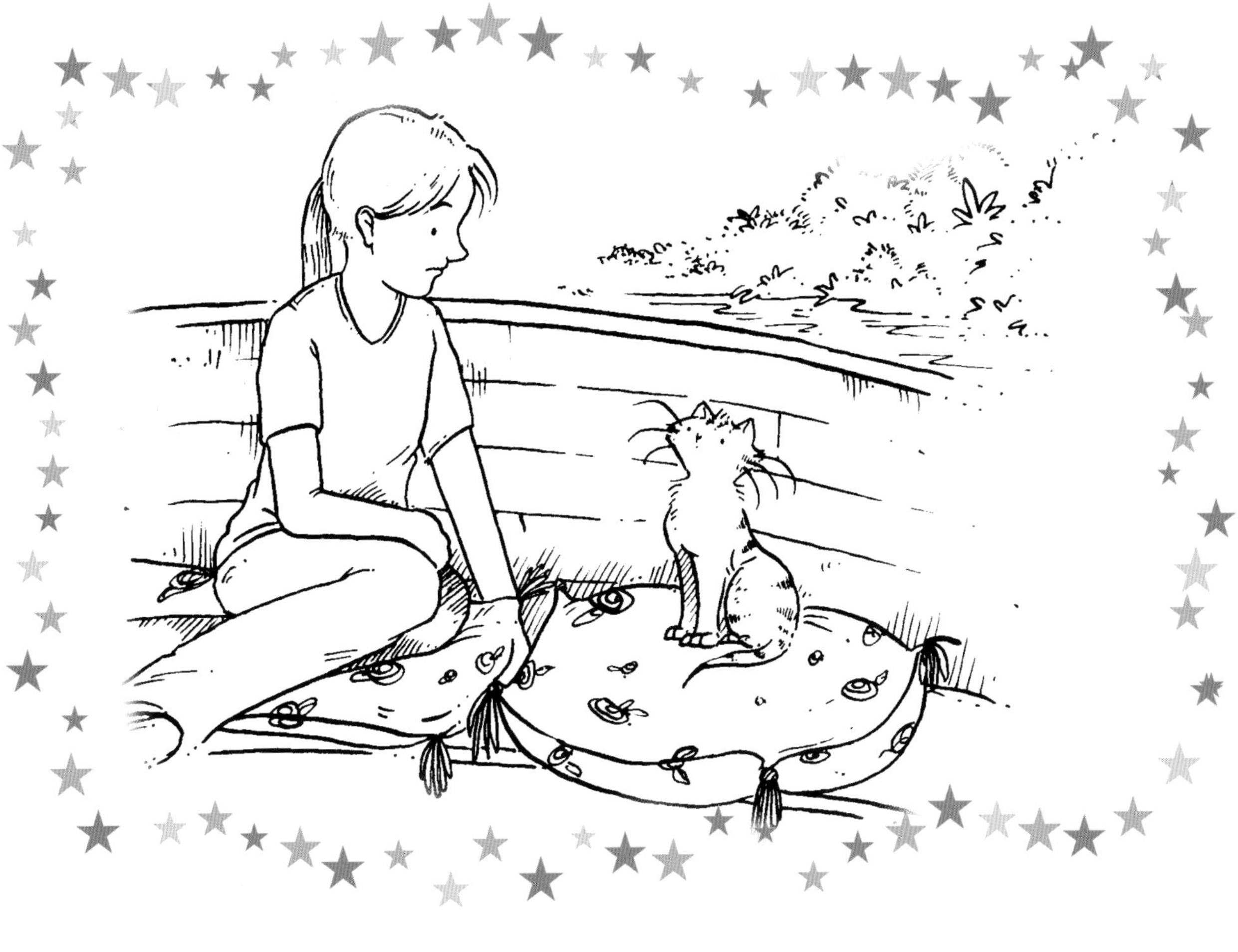

You
see some
friends ahead.
Run forward
two spaces.

Kitten Corners

A game for two to four players.
Make kitten pieces by sticking
the round stickers to cardboard circles.
You will need a die, too.

You stop to
watch some
fox cubs. Miss
a turn.

You fall
off your bike.
Miss a turn.

You fall in the river. Miss a turn.

HOW TO PLAY

Each player places a kitten piece on the matching kitten in the corners. Players take turns throwing the dice and moving in the direction shown by the arrow. If you land on a crown, you get another turn. The first person to get back to their kitten is the winner.

You take a shortcut across the beach. Go forward two spaces.

You get lost in a cave. Miss a turn.

Which Breed of Cat Are You?

Have you ever thought it would be fun to be a cat?
If so, which breed would you be? Take this quiz to find out.

What are you like when you're with your friends?

A) The center of attention—my voice is always the loudest. ☐

B) Laid-back, but happy to join in when I have something to say. ☐

C) Quiet. I'd rather just watch and listen. ☐

How long do you spend doing your hair before school?

A) At least half an hour. ☐

B) I run a comb through it and I'm good to go. ☐

C) I don't even bother to look in the mirror. ☐

On weekends what would you rather do?

A) Go shopping. ☐

B) Get out in the fresh air and get some exercise. ☐

C) Curl up on the couch with a good book. ☐

You hear a group of girls saying mean things about a new girl in your class. What do you do?

A) Listen to what they have to say in case they mention my name. ☐

B) Stand up for the new girl. ☐

C) Go away—I don't want to be drawn into the conversation. ☐

What's your favorite restaurant?

A) The newest place—I like to see and be seen. ☐

B) Anywhere with fast service—I'm always on the run. ☐

C) I'd rather stay at home and get takeout. ☐

Where can you be found during a race in gym class?

A) Getting a tan on the sidelines. Running ruins my hair. ☐

B) First at the finish line. ☐

C) Bringing up the rear. ☐

HOW DID YOU SCORE?

Mostly As:
Siamese

You are demanding and expect attention at all times. You don't like to be left alone and you can get yourself into trouble unless someone, or something, keeps you amused. You have a very loud voice and you like to be heard.

Mostly Bs:
Abyssinian

You are active and playful. Your lively and adventurous nature means you don't sit still for long. You are interested in people and are an affectionate and loyal friend, but you are also happy to entertain yourself if necessary.

Mostly Cs:
British Shorthair

You are quiet, gentle, and undemanding. If there's any sign of trouble, you choose to run and hide rather than get involved. You are not athletic, preferring to keep your feet safely on the ground or—better still—up on the couch.

Kitten Conundrum

Are you as clever as Flame? Can you figure out which kitten completes these line-ups? When you know the answer, place the right sticker over the question mark.

Answers on page 32

The Lion Throne

One day, Prince Flame will seize the Lion Throne from his uncle Ebony. Draw a picture of Flame as a lion on his throne.

Toys for Your Cat

Make special treats for your favorite feline friend.
Ask an adult to help you with the cutting and sewing.

TIP
Keep an eye on your cat's toys. Remove or reattach any small parts that are coming loose.

HOW TO MAKE A FEATHER FISHING ROD

You will need:

A small stick or cane

A length of strong twine (or dental floss)

A few feathers

Two small pieces of sticky tape

1 Tie the feathers together tightly with the twine (or dental floss). Wrap sticky tape around the knotted twine to keep the feathers in place.

2 Tie the other end of the twine to the stick or cane and wrap sticky tape around it to stop it from sliding off the stick. Dangle the feathers in front of your cat's nose, or pull them along the floor.

HOW TO MAKE A CATNIP MOUSE

You will need:

A small sock

Scraps of felt for the ears

Scissors

A teardrop-shaped piece of cardboard

Catnip (from a pet shop)

Some yarn

A needle with an eye large enough to thread the yarn through

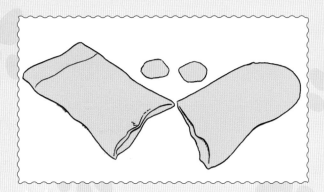

1 Cut off the sock across the heel as shown and cut two circles from the felt to make the ears.

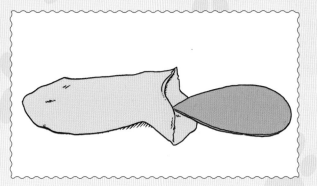

2 Put the piece of cardboard inside the sock to make a mouse shape, and stuff the sock with catnip.

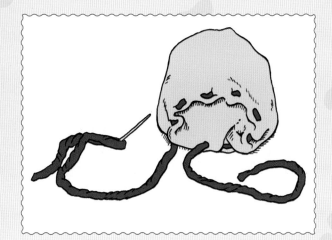

3 Tuck the open end of the sock over the catnip and then use the yarn to stitch around the edge as shown. Pull the yarn tight and tie it securely, leaving a long piece of yarn to form the tail.

4 Sew on the ears—make sure they are attached well so your cat won't swallow them. Then draw or stitch the mouse's eyes and nose.

Friend or Foe?

Unscramble these letters to find the names of some of Flame's friends,
but look out for one of his enemies who is hiding here, too.

RSOIE

_ _ _ _ _

NORAL

_ _ _ _ _

EBNYO

_ _ _ _ _

SIEMIA

_ _ _ _ _ _

DISEA

_ _ _ _ _

VOILIA

_ _ _ _ _ _

ISAL

_ _ _ _

SURCIR

_ _ _ _ _ _

RAAK

_ _ _ _

Answers on page 32

How to Draw Flame

It's easy to draw Flame if you copy this picture, square by square, into the grid below. When you're done, color in your drawing.

Give yourself a star sticker when you have completed your picture.

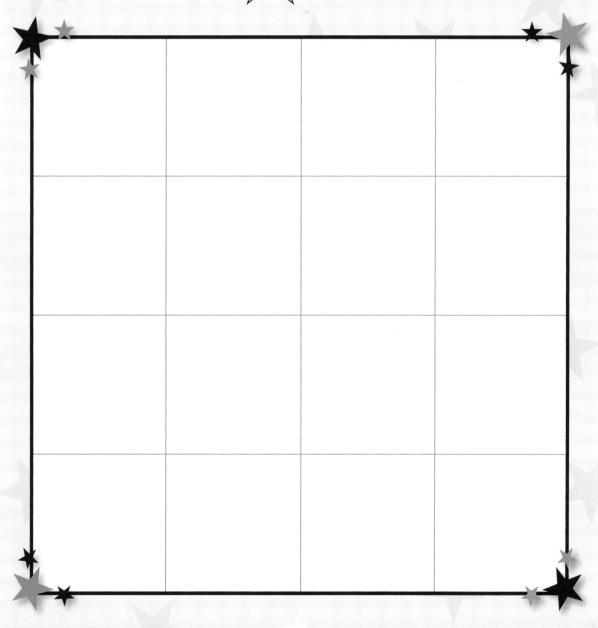

My Purrfect Planner

Use this year planner to keep a note of things to do and dates to remember.

SPRING

Spring is in the air, so it's time to get outside and enjoy the flowers.

My plans for March:

My plans for April:

My plans for May:

Important dates:

Don't forget April Fool's Day on April 1ˢᵗ and Mother's Day in May.

SUMMER

Long summer days mean there's lots of time for lazing in the sun.

My plans for June:

My plans for July:

My plans for August:

Important dates:

Don't forget Father's Day in June.

FALL

Crisp, breezy days are ideal for
playing in the fall leaves.

My plans for September:

My plans for October:

My plans for November:

Important dates:

Don't forget Halloween on October 31st
and Thanksgiving at the end of
November.

What I'm thankful for:

WINTER

When it's cold outside, curl up
on the couch in front of the fire.

My plans for December:

My plans for January:

My plans for February:

Important dates:

Don't forget Christmas on December 25th
and Valentine's Day on February 14th.

My Christmas wish:

Cat Spotter's Diary

Use these pages to keep a note of the cats you see in your neighborhood. That way you will know if a new kitten suddenly appears. Could it be Flame?

Date seen:_____

Location:_____

Coat color:_____

Eye color:_____

Description:_____
_____

Distinguishing features: _____
_____

Rough age:_____

Date seen:_____

Location:_____

Coat color:_____

Eye color:_____

Description:_____
_____

Distinguishing features: _____
_____

Rough age:_____

If you see two similar cats, write down the color of their legs, paws, and tails to tell them apart.

Date seen: _____

Location:_____

Coat color: _____

Eye color:_____

Description: _____
_____

Distinguishing features: _____
_____

Rough age: _____

Make a note of any special features, such as a bushy tail.

Date seen:_____

Location:_____

Coat color:_____

Eye color:_____

Description:_____
_____

Distinguishing features:_____
_____

Rough age:_____

Date seen:_____

Location:_____

Coat color:_____

Eye color:_____

Description:_____

Distinguishing features: _____

Rough age:_____

Date seen: _____
Location: _____
Coat color: _____
Eye color: _____
Description: _____
_____
Distinguishing features: _____
_____
Rough age: _____

Date seen: _____
Location: _____
Coat color: _____
Eye color: _____
Description: _____
Distinguishing features: _____
_____
Rough age: _____

Date seen: _____
Location: _____
Coat color: _____
Eye color: _____
Description: _____
Distinguishing features: _____
_____
Rough age: _____

Date seen: _____
Location: _____
Coat color: _____
Eye color: _____
Description: _____
Distinguishing features: _____
_____
Rough age: _____

Date seen: _____
Location: _____
Coat color: _____
Eye color: _____
Description: _____
Distinguishing features: _____
_____
Rough age: _____

Date seen: _____
Location: _____
Coat color: _____
Eye color: _____
Description: _____
Distinguishing features: _____
Rough age: _____

You could include a sketch of the cat's facial markings.

21

Flame's Friends Word Search

The names of some of Flame's friends have been hidden in this word search.
They might be written forward, backward, up, down, or diagonally.

Lisa   Abi   Zoe   Kim   Jemma   Lorna

L	K	M	E	J	E	M	A	V	A	B	I
B	I	U	C	O	I	Y	J	G	C	E	M
O	K	S	L	R	S	T	E	X	M	I	A
M	A	P	A	E	O	I	M	C	I	S	F
I	R	O	G	S	R	C	M	O	K	M	O
K	A	R	A	L	U	M	A	W	Z	L	P
V	L	U	R	E	A	L	O	E	I	N	L
Z	I	M	J	I	G	J	N	V	O	P	O
E	H	I	M	D	H	D	I	S	A	B	R
K	O	L	S	A	R	A	C	E	E	I	N
M	C	Z	U	S	A	S	I	T	V	C	A
E	I	S	I	A	M	A	K	J	E	N	R

Eve   Kara   Maisie   Olivia   Sadie   Rosie

Answers on page 32

Odd One Out

These pictures of Flame with his friend Olivia may look identical, but one is different than the other three. Can you figure out which one?

A

B

C

D

23

Answer on page 32

Make Magic Kitten Cards

Everyone loves a homemade card, especially when they are as magical as these.
Ask an adult to help you cut the white paper or cardstock to size.

For each card you will need:

A sheet of colored cardstock with an envelope it will fit in when it is folded in two
(or a blank card and envelope from a craft shop)

A piece of white paper the size of the pictures opposite

Paints, markers, colored pencils, crayons

Glue

Sequins, stickers, and/or glitter to decorate

TIP
Make sure the glue is completely dry and slide the cards very carefully into the envelopes so the sequins don't come off.

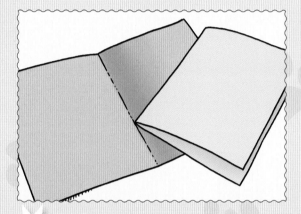

1 Fold each colored card in two.

2 Write your message inside each card.

3 Photocopy or trace the pictures on the opposite page onto the white paper, then color and glue them to the front of your cards.

4 Decorate your cards with sequins, stickers, and/or glitter so they sparkle with magic.

Magic Kitten Sudoku

Cats are said to have nine lives, so Flame should enjoy this puzzle based on the number nine—however, you will need logic, rather than magic, to solve it.

HOW TO PLAY:

The numbers one to nine should appear only once in each column, row, and shaded square. Some numbers have already been entered, so all you have to do is fill in the gaps.

3		5	9		6			1
	6	2	1		3		5	
8	7		4	5		9		3
		4		3		7	9	6
7	3		6		1		8	5
5	8	6		9		1		
1	2			8			4	9
		8	3		9		7	
6	9		5	2	4	3		8

TIP
Start with a row or column in which a lot of numbers have been filled in, and write in pencil, so you can erase any mistakes.

Give yourself a star sticker when you have completed the puzzle.

Answers on page 32

Supersenses

Not every cat can perform magic like Flame, but they
all have very special skills.

★ ★ HEARING ★ ★

Cats' ears are designed to pinpoint the faintest
sounds. They can locate the rustling of a mouse
in the long grass from the other side of the
garden, and they can hear high-pitched sounds
far beyond the range of humans and even dogs.

Their ears are like mini satellite dishes that can
rotate up to 180 degrees in the direction of a
sound. They can hear things five times farther
away than we can—so if you think your cat
has a sixth sense when it goes to the door before
you hear someone coming, it's just because it
heard their footsteps long before you did!

★ ★ SMELL ★ ★

A cat's sense of smell is fourteen times better
than ours. This is how cats recognize people
and objects. Cats mark their homes and
owners by rubbing them with scent from their
bodies. A cat can "taste" smells in the roof
of its mouth, so you may see your cat opening
its mouth and breathing in when it picks up
an interesting scent.

★ ★ TASTE ★ ★

Members of the cat family can't taste sweet
things—so you are unlikely to find your cat
stealing your stash of chocolate!

★ ★ TOUCH ★ ★

Cats' whiskers are supersensitive. They pick
up the tiniest change in the way the air moves.
This is why cats don't bump into things, even
in the dark. They can feel the difference in the
air currents around objects. A cat's whiskers
are about the same width as its body, so they
are like a ruler, allowing the cat to measure
whether its body will fit.

★ ★ SIGHT ★ ★

During the day, cats can't see as well as we
can and rely on their noses more than their eyes,
but at night the tables are turned. When it
gets dark, the part of the cat's eye that lets the
light in opens wider than ours, so they can
see better than us.

Dream Time

Cats sleep for up to sixteen hours a day. You can often see their paws and tails twitching as they dream of chasing imaginary mice. Find the sticker of Flame asleep on Lisa's bed and draw a picture of what he might be dreaming about.

Place sticker here

The Meaning of Dreams

We dream for an average of two hours a night, which adds up to six years of our lives. Dreams can be fun—or sometimes frightening—but what do they mean?

★★ ANIMALS ★★

Animals often appear in dreams. Cats are thought to bring good or bad luck, so dreaming about them could mean something magical is going to happen. Dogs may turn up in your dreams as a guide, leading you somewhere you have never been before. This could show that you are about to enter a different stage in your life. If you dream of exploring unknown places on horseback, this might be because you want to travel and learn something new.

★★ COLORS ★★

The color of something you see in your dreams can be as important as the object itself. The color white is a sign of hope and shows that people can rely on you. Green means you are happy and take pleasure in simple things. Orange shows you have drive and ambition, and yellow is a sign of confidence and intelligence. Brown means you are practical and down-to-earth, and blue is a symbol of peace. Red stands for passion and joy, and pink for love and tenderness.

★★ FALLING ★★

Falling dreams usually happen just after you have gone to sleep, and often make your body jerk and twitch, waking you up again. They are said to mean that you are feeling helpless and are worried about losing control.

★★ FLYING ★★

Flying dreams are a sign that you have a good imagination and are happy with your life. Perhaps you are proud of something you have achieved. This is usually an enjoyable dream and you may remember the feeling of fun and freedom for weeks afterward.

★★ TAKING A TEST ★★

Have you ever dreamed that you have arrived late for a test, that your pen doesn't work, or that you don't understand the questions? Such dreams may mean that you feel you are being judged by other people and do not live up to their expectations, or that you feel unprepared for something. Perhaps you need to have more confidence in yourself. Don't underestimate your abilities, and don't worry—it is very unlikely that you will fail a test in real life just because everything went wrong in your dream.

My Magic Kitten Story

It's time to write your own Magic Kitten adventure! Complete this story, illustrating it with stickers where shown. Add your own drawings, then color the pictures.

Write the title of your story here.

____ by ______________________

1

Place sticker here

Sitting on a rock was a brown tabby kitten with the brightest emerald-green eyes.

2

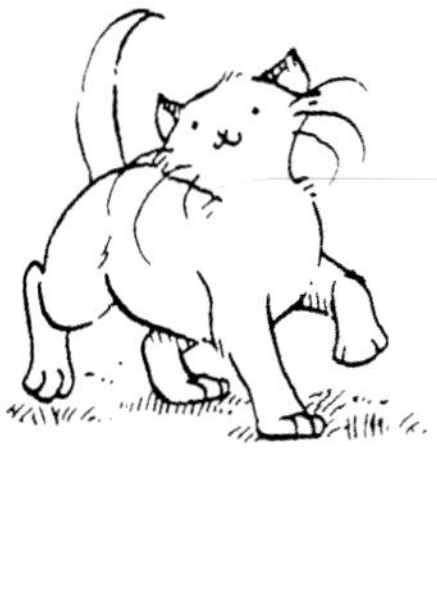

3

_____

_____

4

Place sticker
here

The cave was dark and spooky. -

- -

5

_____

_____

Answers

Page 12 Kitten Conundrum
The missing kittens are:

Page 16 Friend or Foe?
The names of Flame's friends are Rosie; Lorna; Maisie; Sadie; Olivia; Lisa; Cirrus; Kara.
The name of Flame's enemy is Ebony.

Page 22 Flame's Friends Word Search

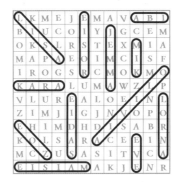

Page 23 Odd One Out
C: Olivia's shoe is a different color.

Page 26 Magic Kitten Sudoku

3	4	5	9	7	6	8	2	1
9	6	2	1	8	3	4	5	7
8	7	1	4	5	2	9	6	3
2	1	4	8	3	5	7	9	6
7	3	9	6	4	1	2	8	5
5	8	6	2	9	7	1	3	4
1	2	3	7	6	8	5	4	9
4	5	8	3	1	9	6	7	2
6	9	7	5	2	4	3	1	8

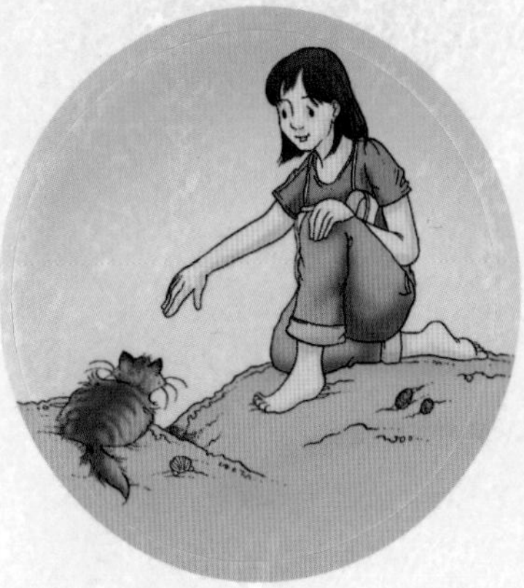
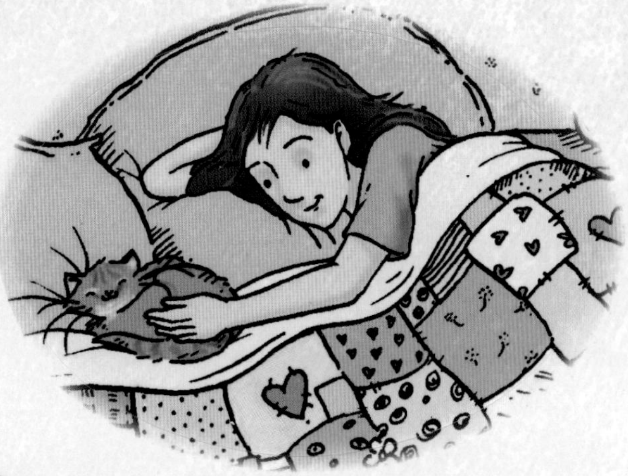
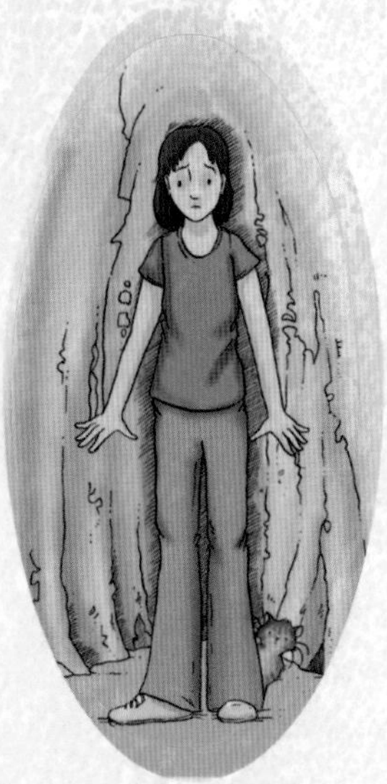
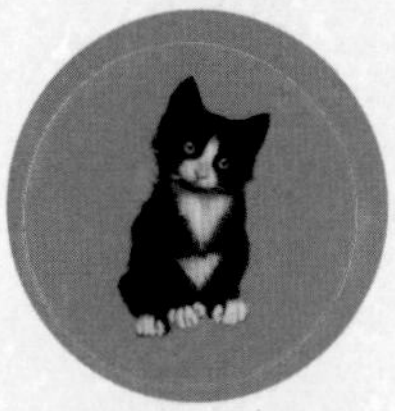
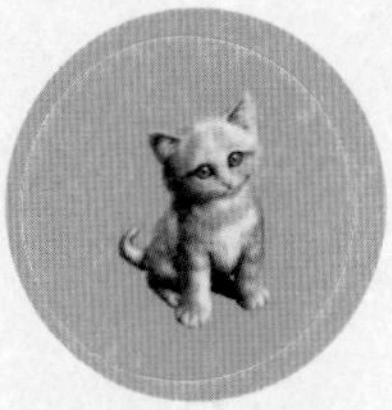
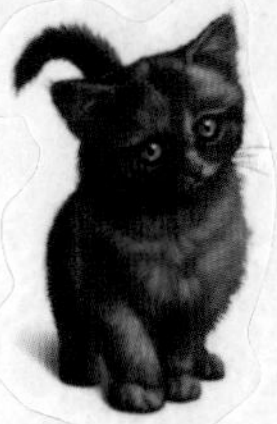
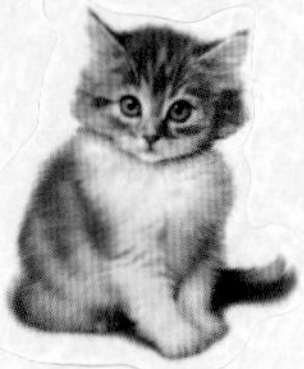
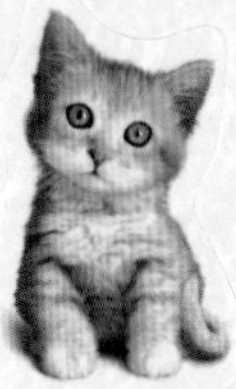
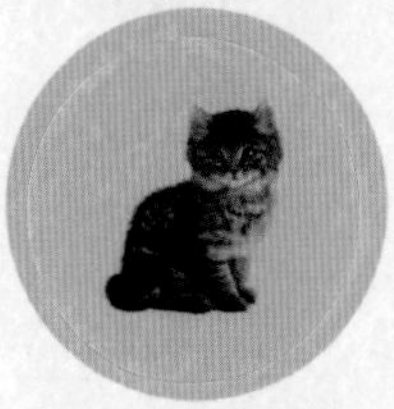
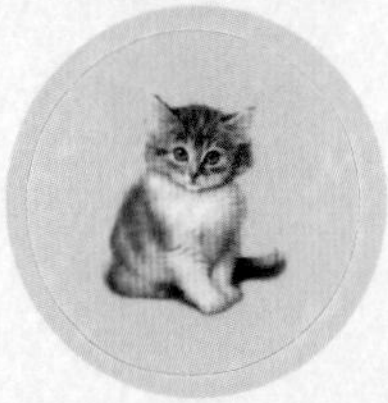
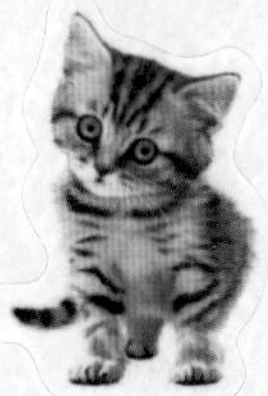
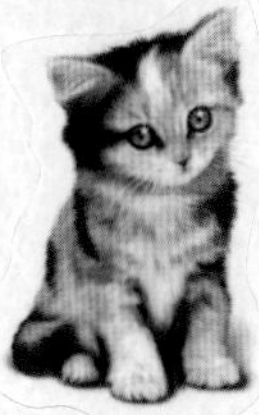

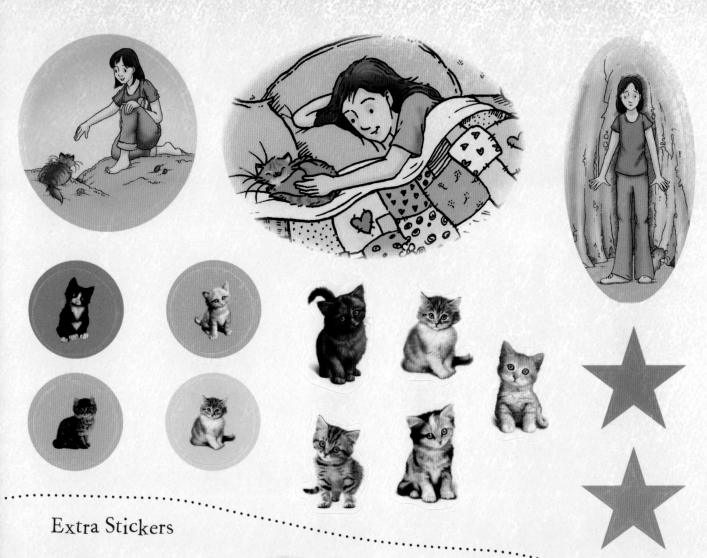

Extra Stickers

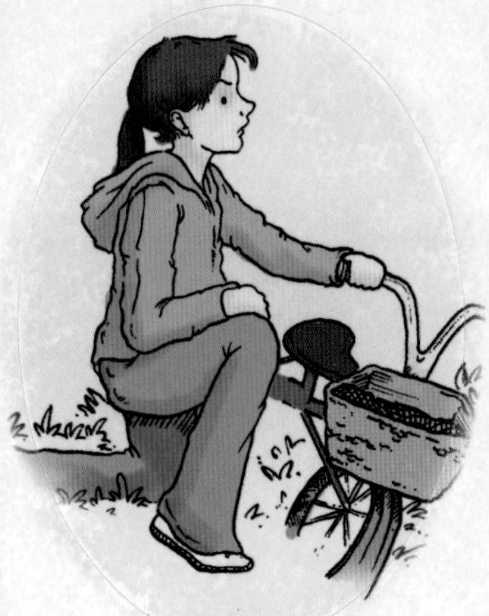
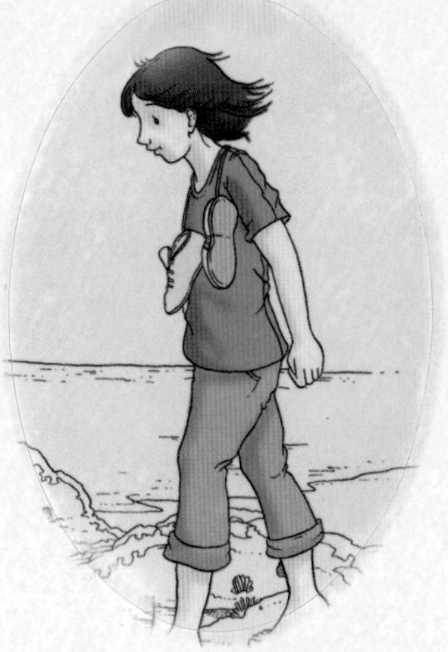
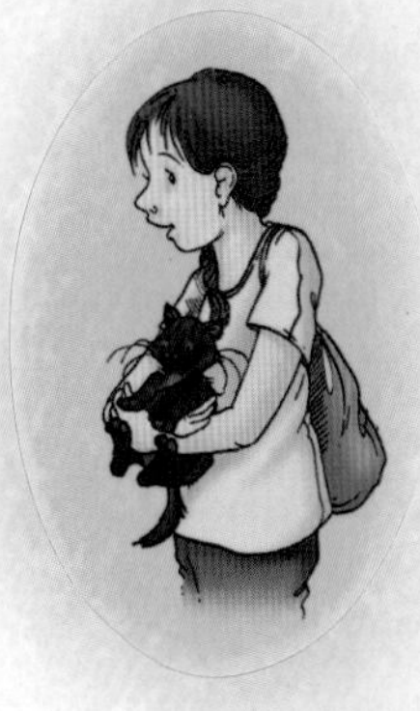
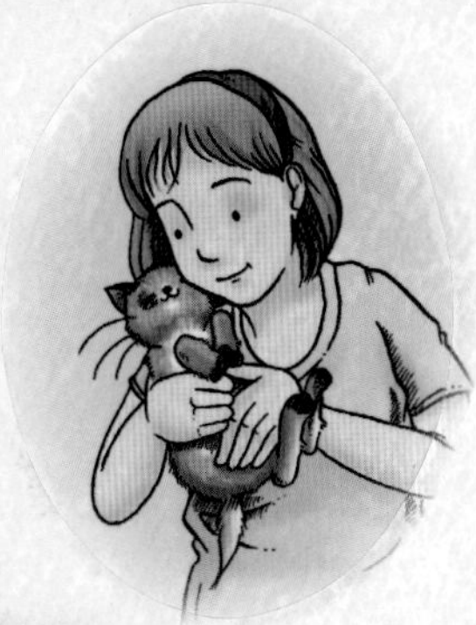
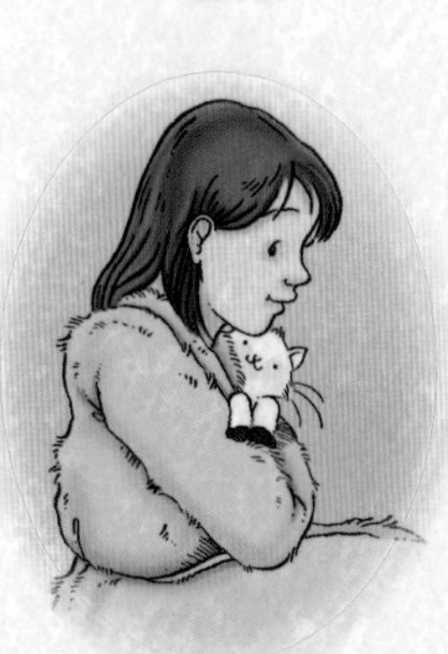
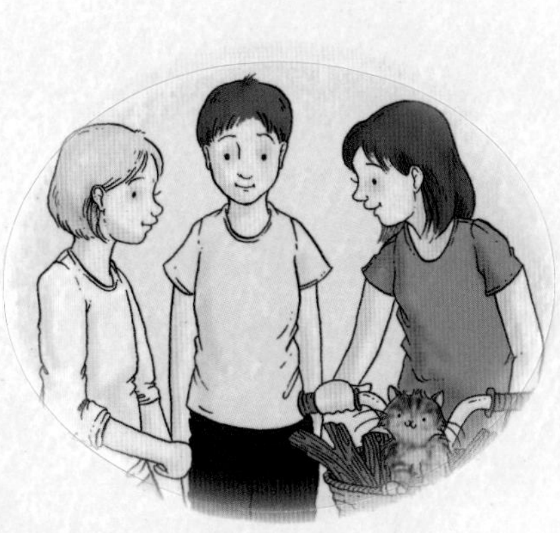
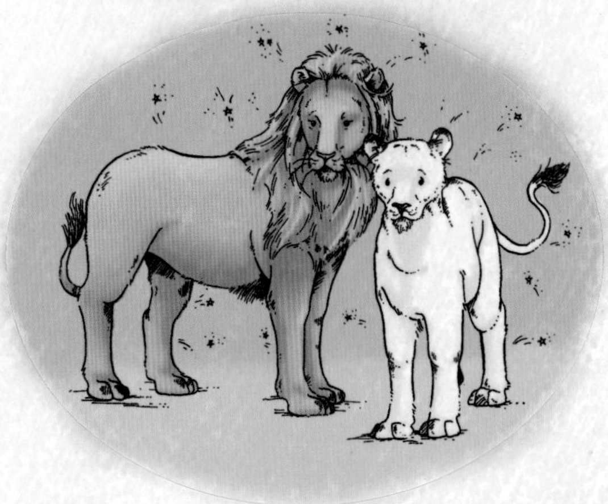

Extra Stickers

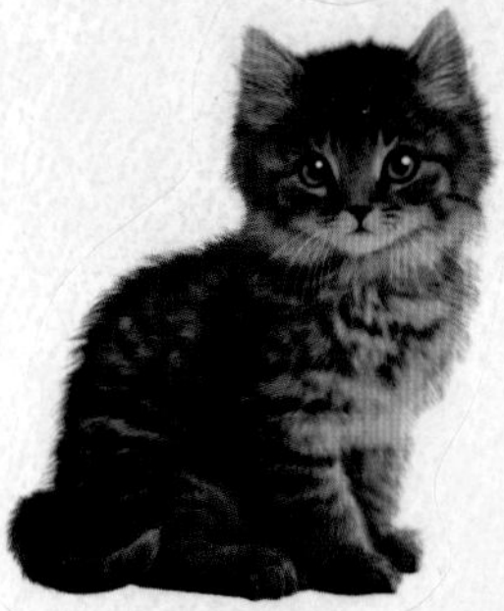
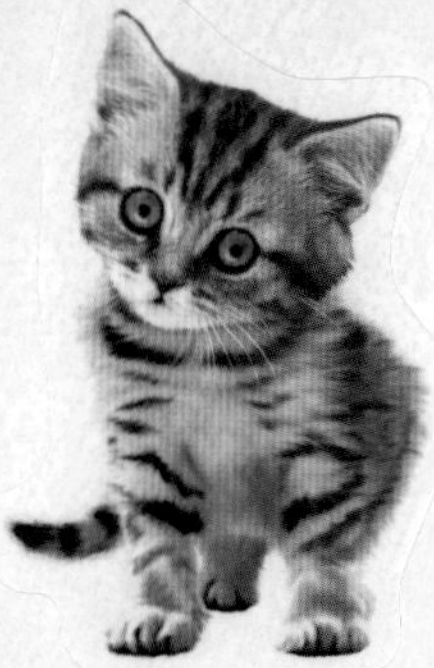
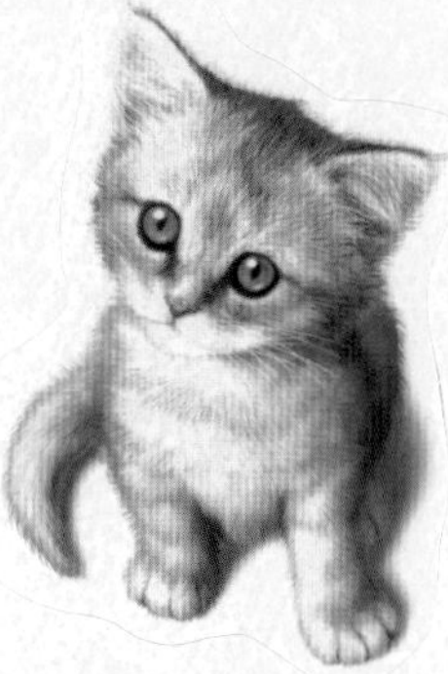
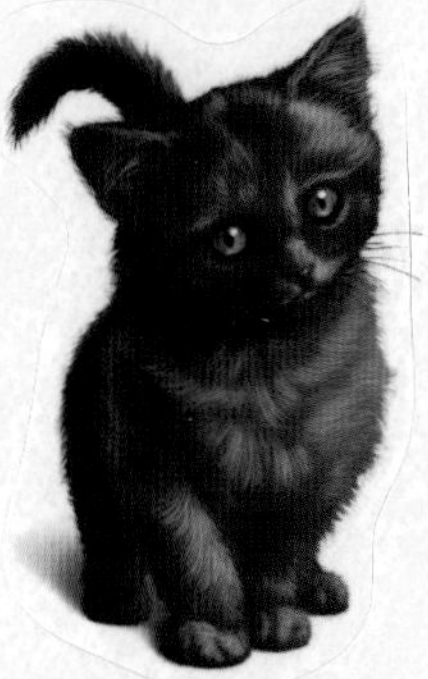
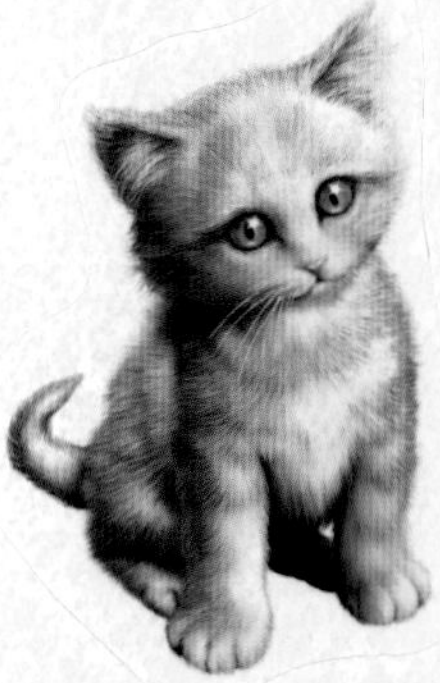
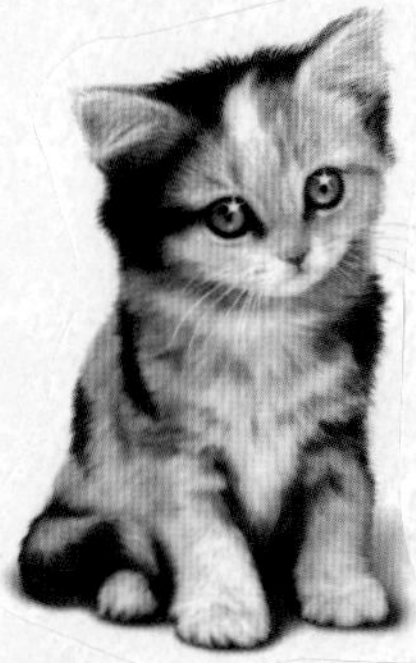
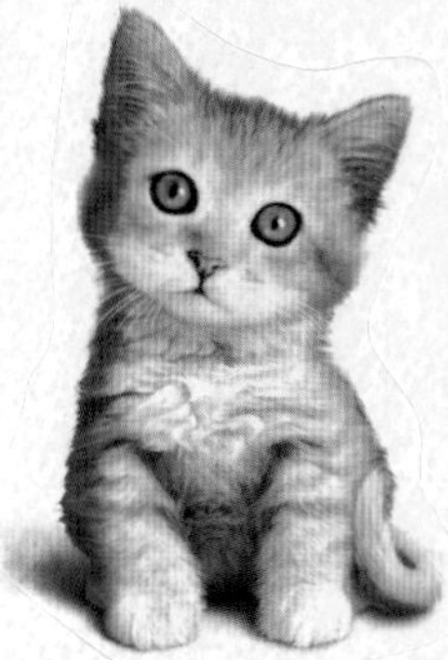
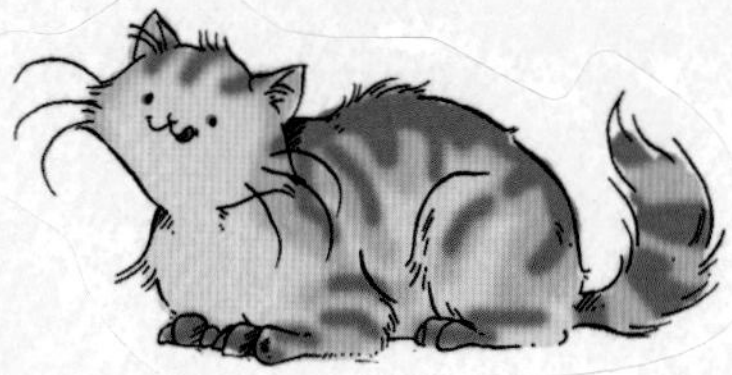
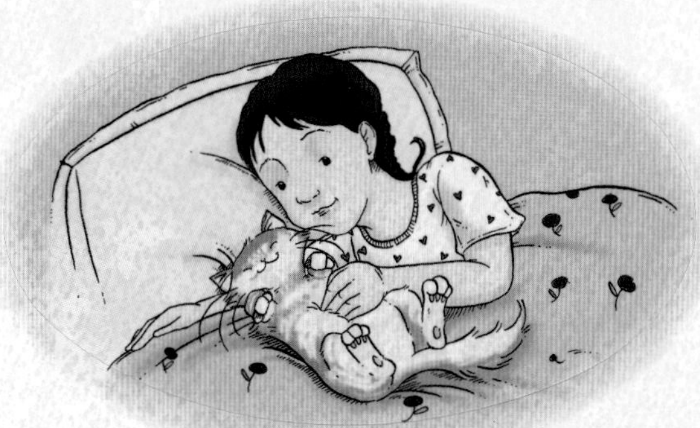

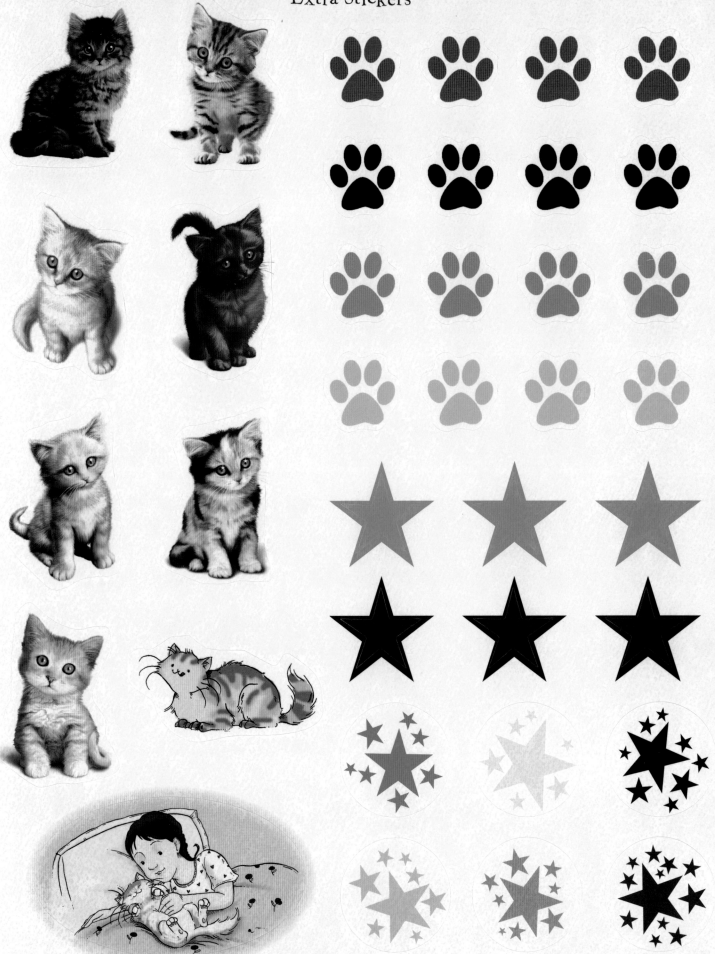